WITHDRAWN

For Fiona

100 School Days
Text copyright © 2002 by Anne Rockwell
Illustrations copyright © 2002 by Lizzy Rockwell
Manufactured in China. All rights reserved. No part of this book may be used
or reproduced in any manner whatsoever without written permission except in the
case of brief quotations embodied in critical articles and reviews. For information
address HarperCollins Children's Books, a division of HarperCollins Publishers,
1350 Avenue of the Americas, New York, NY 10019.
www.harperchildrens.com

Library of Congress Cataloging-in-Publication Data   Rockwell, Anne F.   100 school days /
story by Anne Rockwell ; pictures by Lizzy Rockwell.   p.   cm.
Summary: The students in Mrs. Madoff's class keep track of the days they have been
in school, marking each interval of ten, until they reach 100 days.
ISBN 0-06-029144-3 — ISBN 0-06-029145-1 (lib. bdg.) — ISBN 0-06-443727-2 (pbk.)
[1. Schools—Fiction.   2. Hundred (The number)—Fiction.]
I. Title: One hundred school days.   II. Rockwell, Lizzy, ill.   III. Title.
PZ7.R5943 Aac   2002   00-040704   [E]—dc21   CIP   AC

Typography by Elynn Cohen
❖

100 School Days

story by **Anne Rockwell**

pictures by **Lizzy Rockwell**

HarperCollinsPublishers

On the first day of school
Mrs. Madoff gave me a penny.
She asked me to put it in the jar on her desk.
Plink! I dropped the penny into the jar.
Mrs. Madoff asked Evan to bring
a penny to school the next day.

Every day someone put a penny in the jar.
Plink! Plink! Plink!
Every day we helped count the pennies.
Mrs. Madoff told us that's how we would know
how many days we had gone to school.

When we counted 10 pennies,
we knew we'd been going to school for 10 days.
But we'd learned more than 10 new things!

HOW MUCH IS 100?

1	2	3	4	5	6	7	8	9	10
11	12	13	14	15	16	17	18	19	20
21	22	23	24	25	26	27	28	29	30
31	32	33	34	35	36	37	38	39	40
41	42	43	44	45	46	47	48	49	50
51	52	53	54	55	56	57	58	59	60
61	62	63	64	65	66	67	68	69	70
71	72	73	74	75	76	77	78	79	80
81	82	83	84	85	86	87	88	89	90
91	92	93	94	95	96	97	98	99	100

On Day 10 *Plink!* Sam put his penny in the jar.
He also brought 10 balloons to celebrate Day 10.
Each of us blew up 1 balloon.
Then Sam and I took them to the principal's office.
She said, "Thank you! These are beautiful!"

Plink! went the penny Evan
dropped into the jar.
When we counted them,
we found 20 pennies.
We knew it was Day 20.
That's why Evan brought
20 Matchbox cars to school.

When Day 30 came,
Michiko dropped in her penny.
It went *Plink!* when it landed
on top of the pennies in the jar.
She had collected 30 red, brown,
and yellow leaves.
We taped them to the windows of
our classroom to celebrate autumn.

On Day 40 Sarah brought in a penny, and *Plink!*—
she dropped it into the jar.
She brought 40 paperback books to school.
Her grandmother helped her carry them,
because they were heavy.

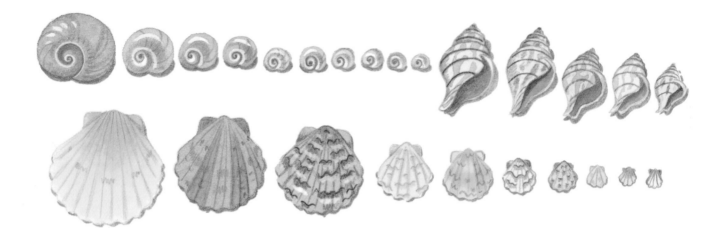

On Day 50 Eveline brought in a penny.
She dropped it with a *Plink!* into the jar.
She also brought 50 seashells to school
and told us how she had collected them
at the beach.

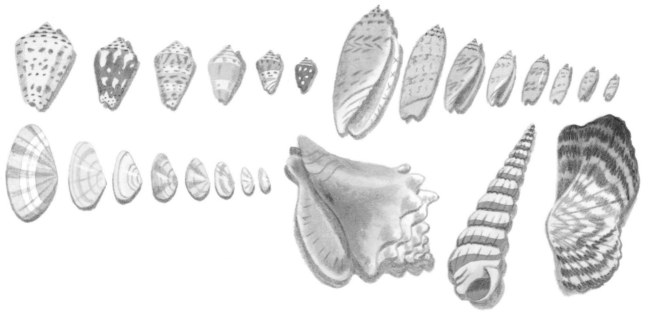

On Day 60 Nicholas dropped in his penny.
Plink! It landed in the penny jar.
It took a long time to count the pennies.
Nicholas brought 60 baseball trading cards
with pictures of famous ball players on them.
He said he went to 4 baseball games
during summer vacation
and saw Lonnie Alonzo hit 2 home runs.

On Day 70 it was so cold and windy outside,
I wore the woolly hat that covers my ears.
That day Kate dropped a penny into the jar
with a *Plink!*
She also brought in 70 sunflower seeds.
We made a sunflower cake and put it
in a string bag for the hungry birds.

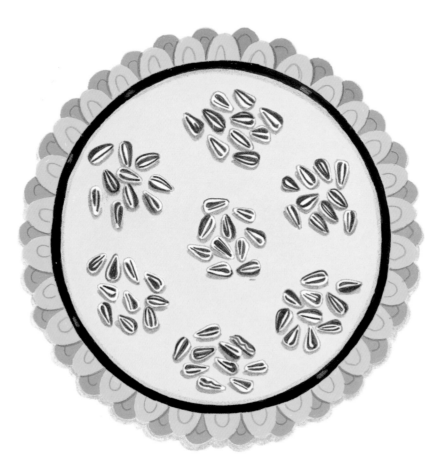

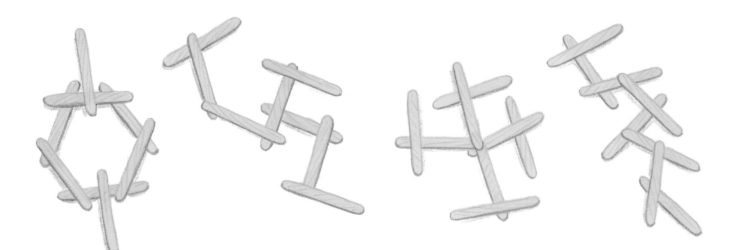

When Day 80 came, Pablo brought in a penny.
Plink! it went as he dropped it into the jar.
That morning we counted 80 pennies.
Pablo also brought a package
of 80 Popsicle sticks to school.
We each got 8 sticks.
Look what I made with mine!

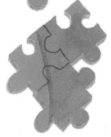

On Day 90 Charlie brought in a penny.
Plink! it went.
The jar of pennies was almost full!
Charlie brought a puzzle with 90 pieces.
He told me he'd already put the puzzle together
and made a picture of a dinosaur.
Then he took it apart again.

Finally the big day arrived.
It was Day 100!
That day I brought in a penny.
Plink! The jar was full.
We counted 100 pennies.
That meant we'd been going to school
for 100 days.

I brought 100 jelly beans to celebrate Day 100.
Everyone brought a bag that held

of something good to eat.
There were

100 pretzels,

100 pieces of popcorn,

100 raisins,

100 almonds,

100 chocolate chips,

100 pieces of star-shaped cereal,

100 mini marshmallows,

100 dried banana chips,

100 cheesy fish crackers,

and 100 smooth jelly beans.

We took turns passing the bowl of yummy treats to everyone in the cafeteria.

It was Day 100 at my school,
and at all the schools in the city where I live.
Now all those schools are going to send
their jars of 100 pennies far away.
They're sending the money to the town
where the hurricane hit.

The people who live in that town can buy
something they need with all those pennies.
I wonder what it will be.